Secrets

of the

Rain Forest

Betty Frost

ORDER DIRECTLY FROM
ANN ARBOR PUBLISHERS
P.O. BOX 1
BELFORD
NORTHUMBERLAND NE70 7JX

Cover Design and Illustrations: Herb Heidinger

International Standard Book Number: 0-87879-321-6

1 0 9 8 7 6
0 9 8 7 6 5 4 3

You'll enjoy all the High Noon Books.
Write for a free full list of titles.

Contents

Chapter 1

Change of Plans

Steve Marshall picked up the letter from the mailbox on his way into the house. He could tell it was from his dad. It had to be. Who else would send a letter with all those strange stamps on it? His father didn't write very often. That was OK with Steve. When Steve's dad, Bill, was home, it was always, "Do this" or "Do that." When he wrote, it was always the same thing.

Steve took the letter out of the envelope. Now what did his dad want? An airplane ticket fell out on to the floor. Steve picked it up and looked at it carefully. It was a one-way ticket to a city in Prima Vera.

Prima Vera? Prima Vera? Where's that? Bill Marshall was always away on one job or another. Steve remembered that this time it was in Prima Vera. But where's that? He got his dad's map book off the shelf. There it is. Near Mexico.

What a small country, Steve thought.

Bill Marshall had been away on that job for almost a year. He was in charge of building a dam for that small country. He was in charge of the big machines and all the men. He had to see that the dam was finished before he could leave.

Steve opened the letter and read it. It was short. Bill Marshall told Steve to come to Prima Vera right away. He said he would meet Steve at the airport at Avila on Wednesday. Wednesday? That was only two days away.

That's my dad, Steve thought. When he says "Jump!" I'm supposed to jump.

Steve went to the phone and called Brad, his best friend.

"Brad, call off that camping trip. I can't make it," he said.

"You can't make it? What's going on? I'm all set for it," Brad said.

"I just got a letter from my father. It was short. He sent me an airplane ticket. I have to meet him in Prima Vera on Wednesday," Steve answered.

"Prima Vera? Isn't that a little country near Mexico?" Brad asked.

"Yeah. That's where my dad has been for almost a year. He's been working on a dam down

2

there," Steve answered.

"Are you going?" Brad asked.

"Am I going? I have to go. You know my dad. Do this. Do that. Do this. Do that," Steve answered.

"Can't you get out of it?" Brad asked.

"No way," Steve answered. "My dad never

"Can't you get out of it?" Brad asked.
"No way," Steve answered.

3

changes his mind. When it's made up, it's made up."

"How long will you be there?" Brad asked.

"He sent a one-way ticket. So you know I'm not going to be right back," Steve answered.

"Take care. Write and let me know how it's going down there," Brad said.

"Will do," Steve answered.

Steve put the phone down. Then he sat down. Bill Marshall had done it again. Steve's summer was ruined.

He started to get things ready to leave. He got a small suitcase and put clothes in it. Why did he have to get that letter, he thought.

Two days to get ready wasn't much time. Steve had a lot to do. But before he knew it, he was packed and at the airport waiting to get on the plane for Prima Vera.

Prima Vera. Prima Vera. Steve wondered what it would be like.

Chapter 2

Arrival in Prima Vera

Steve had fallen asleep. The sound of the airplane's flaps coming down woke him. The "fasten your seat belt" sign flashed on. The book he had started to read was still open on his lap. He put it away. Then he pulled his seat belt tight. The plane slowly started down to the airport. Steve looked out of the window. All he could see for miles and miles was jungle and mountains. Then he saw Avila, the capital of Prima Vera.

The plane smoothly touched ground. It had been a long trip but a good one. He was tired. He had started out in the morning. Now it was late in the afternoon. He got his small suitcase out from under the seat. People started to stand and get their things. Why rush, he thought. Let everyone else get off first.

When he got to the door of the plane, he stopped. Steve Marshall was tall like his dad. He spotted Bill right away. As he walked down from the plane to get to the gate, he was thinking about what he would say to his father.

Bill smiled when Steve shook his hand. Steve had grown. He wasn't a little kid any more. Bill looked at him for a minute. He's as big as I am, he thought.

"Come on," Bill said. "I have a car ready for us."

Bill led Steve to a small blue car with a man sitting in it. Steve was surprised.

"A driver? How come?" Steve asked.

Bill opened the door for Steve. "Get in," he said.

Pedro, the driver, started the car.

"When we started work on the dam, we said we would hire as many people from Prima Vera as we could. Pedro is a good driver. He knows most of the roads in the whole country. I needed someone like him. He's a big help," Bill said.

"Dad, we need to do some talking," Steve said.

"I know we do. A lot of it. But not now. Wait," Bill said.

Then Bill said, "Pedro, this is my son, Steve."

"Pleased to meet you, Pedro," Steve said.

Fifteen minutes later Pedro stopped the car in front of a long trailer.

"Well, here it is. Our home," Bill said.

They both got out and went inside. Pedro called out, "I'll be back in the morning, Mr. Bill." He drove away.

"This is home and office," Bill said. "The dam is over the hill. You'll see it tomorrow. Are you hungry?"

Steve looked around the trailer. He sat down and said, "I had a little to eat on the plane. Yes, I am hungry. But, Dad, I want to talk first."

"OK. OK. Then dinner," Bill said. "Now, what's on your mind?"

"Dad, ever since I was a kid you've said, 'Come here,' 'Go there,' like I was some kind of a toy," Steve said.

"What's bugging you?" Bill said.

"I'm not a kid any more," Steve said.

Bill looked at Steve. Everything was quiet for a moment.

"You're right, Steve. You aren't a kid," Bill said.

"So why did you have me come to Prima Vera?" Steve asked.

"All my life I've been working on these jobs all over the world," Bill said.

"That's right. You'd be home for a few weeks. Then you'd leave for months. Before Mom died she said she hardly knew you anymore," Steve said.

"That's why I wanted you here, Steve. I want you to know me better. I want to know you better. I knew you wanted to camp this summer. But I needed to spend time here with you," Bill said.

"Doing what?" Steve asked.

"See what I'm doing. Learn about my work. Maybe you'll like it," Bill said.

"Well, I already know you're building a dam," Steve said.

"Steve, this is more than just a dam. These people need this dam. This country is poor. But it has good soil. There could be many farms. But water is needed in the warm months. When this dam is finished, there will be water — plenty of it," Bill said. "Power, too, for electricity."

Steve was listening. He had never heard his dad talk this way. Bill wasn't just talking about a dam or a bridge or a factory, but about people and helping them.

"Tell me more, Dad. I like what you're saying," Steve said.

"Steve, let me tell you about Prima Vera. A long time ago, the Mayan Indians who lived here built great buildings. They knew about the rain and how to save water for the dry season.

They had farms and grew corn. They had great cities, larger than many of ours back home."

Steve listened to Bill. It didn't seem that there could ever have been great cities in the jungles of Prima Vera.

"That was a long time ago," Bill said. "They have been finding some of the buildings of these great cities right in the jungle, all covered by trees. There is so much rain that trees grow very fast and can cover anything almost before you know it."

"You mean some of those buildings are still around?" Steve asked.

"Yes, they are. In fact, there are some people who are digging in the jungle right now. They are looking for the palace of the last great Mayan king. You'll meet them. They are digging a few miles from the dam," Bill said.

"Tell me more," Steve said. He liked talking this way with his dad. They had never done it before.

Bill could see that Steve no longer seemed so angry. He kept on talking. "No one knows what happened, Steve. There was a great king. He was very wise. He was fair. But when he died, the men under him fought to take over the country. They think there was a bad war. The Indians left the cities and went back into the jungles. They never came back to the cities."

"And now you are helping the people of Prima Vera to have water again," Steve said.

"It will take years after the dam is finished. But it will start them off," Bill said. "Even after we're done, they must clear the jungle and start their farms."

Steve looked at his dad. Suddenly he was proud of him. Why didn't they ever talk like this before, he wondered.

"Well, Steve, ready for some dinner?" Bill asked.

"You bet I am," Steve answered. Then he looked at his watch. "Dad! We've been talking for two hours."

"Yeah. Time goes fast when you like the people you're with," Bill said.

Chapter 3

Trouble on the Job

When Steve woke up the next morning, he heard birds and the sounds of the jungle. It all seemed loud. He sat up in his bed. It took him a minute to figure out where he was. He looked at his watch. It was just after 6:00 a.m.

"Are you awake?" Bill asked as he looked in on Steve. Bill was up, dressed, and drinking a cup of coffee.

"How early do you start work out here?" Steve asked.

"We have to start by seven. It gets too hot in the afternoon to work late in the day. It's cool now. Wait until around noon," Bill answered.

Steve jumped up and out of bed. Back home he would have slept until late. But he wanted to prove to his dad that he meant what he said last night.

"What about breakfast?" Steve called out to

Bill. "As usual, I'm starved!"

"Oh, we go down to mess hall for that," Bill answered.

"People working here come from all over the world. That's why we all eat together," Bill said.

Everything looked different in daylight. As they walked to the mess hall, Steve saw people coming and going. He didn't know that there were so many people working on the dam.

"It's like a little city, Steve. This whole place was built just so a lot of people would have somewhere to live while they were working on the dam. Once the dam is finished, it all will be given to the farmers," Bill said.

In the mess hall Bill and Steve got food and sat at a big table with several men. Bill introduced them all to Steve. "Don't worry about getting names straight at first," he said. "In a few days you'll know everyone."

As they were finishing their meal, Pedro ran into the hall. He was out of breath. "They need you, Mr. Bill. There is big trouble. I have the car ready."

"Of course, Pedro. I'll be right there," Bill said as he got up.

"Do you want us to go with you?" asked Dick Townes.

"No, that's OK," Bill said. "I get these calls all the time. Some of these heavy machines are tricky until you get used to them." He turned to his son. "Steve, why don't you go over to the social hall? It's just across the street. I'm sure there will be some young people there. I'll see you later."

When Steve entered the social hall, he found only one young woman. She was turning the pages of a magazine. She looked up and smiled. "Hi, I'm Maria Valli from Milan. That's in Italy. You must be Mr. Marshall's son," she added.

Steve smiled back. "Hi, you're right. I'm Steve Marshall. Do you work here?"

"Yes and no," Maria said. "I don't work for the company that is building the dam. I'm here to join a group that is digging."

Steve looked puzzled. "Digging?"

"We're looking for ruins and things left by the Mayans," Maria answered. "If we can dig up things they made and built, we'll know more about them."

Steve listened carefully. "I don't know a thing about digging," he said.

Maria closed her magazine. "This would be a great place for you to learn. I'm working with Professor Alvarez. He's from the university. He

13

brought some students here to dig, and he lets me tag along."

"I may not know much about digging," Steve joked, "but I've got a strong back to help carry anything you might find."

"That's important, too," Maria said. "Would you really like to go with us?"

"Sure would," said Steve. "I'll have to check with my dad. I don't think he'll mind."

Maria got up and walked to the door. "Meet me in the mess hall tomorrow after breakfast. I'll clear it with Professor Alvarez. I'm sure it will be OK with him, too. See you tomorrow, Steve."

A mile away Bill Marshall frowned. Pedro had been right. There was big trouble. A huge power shovel was hanging on the edge of a cliff. One track of the shovel rested on solid earth. That was a break. But the other track hung in mid air.

If the big rig tipped over, it would fall 300 feet down into the canyon.

"How in the world did this happen?" Bill asked the man standing next to him.

Johnny Ross scratched his head. "It just took a second, Mr. Marshall. One minute I was sitting in the cab. The next minute a bunch of those huge rocks broke loose. That big one over there knocked the shovel sideways and pinned it down.

I was scared! I couldn't get out of there fast enough."

"Good boy, Johnny," Bill said. "You used your head. It was a smart move to lower the shovel's bucket down to the ground. That's what kept it from sliding over the cliff."

Bill walked around the shovel and began to give orders. "We'll need two tractors to move that heavy shovel. And we'll need a couple of pieces of strong cable."

The men hurried away and were soon back with two tractors and some thick cable. Bill picked up a piece of cable and walked toward the shovel. The loose rock made it hard to walk. Once he stumbled and fell to one knee. He climbed up onto the big shovel. It was tilted at a crazy angle. It felt as if he were fifty feet up in the air.

As soon as he was able to stand up straight, Bill looped one end of the cable around the shovel and threw the other end to Johnny. Johnny hooked it onto a tractor. Then Bill hooked up the second cable and threw the end to Pedro.

"Pedro," he called, "hook it up to the other tractor."

The men had to work very carefully. Johnny

and Pedro started the engines of the tractors. Inch by inch the huge shovel began to move away from the edge of the cliff. Finally it was back on the road.

The men stood talking. "Boy, I'm glad that's over," Johnny said. "I thought I was a goner when that thing headed for the cliff."

Bill slapped him lightly on the back. "You used your head, Johnny. You saved an expensive machine."

Johnny laughed. "I don't think I was thinking about the machine. I was thinking about my own neck!"

"You'll be on the job tomorrow, won't you?" Bill asked.

"Sure," Johnny said. "It's like getting back on a horse that has thrown you."

The three men shook hands. Nothing else needed to be said. It was all part of the job.

Chapter 4

The Accident

When Steve woke up the next morning, his father was already gone. He dressed quickly and headed for the mess hall.

He learned about saving the shovel at breakfast. Everyone in the mess hall was talking about it.

"Your father is a hero," Maria said. "He climbed up on that shovel. Johnny Ross said it could have gone over the cliff at any minute."

"He never said a word to me," Steve answered. "I was asleep when he got in. And I was still asleep when he left for the job this morning."

"If you have finished breakfast, let's go," Maria said. "I spoke with Professor Alvarez, and he says it's OK for you to come along. I have a jeep waiting outside."

Steve pushed back his chair and stood up. "I'm ready. Let's go. I didn't see my father. But I'm sure he won't mind."

Maria got into the driver's seat. They drove the jeep over dusty roads to the edge of the jungle. Professor Alvarez was waiting for them. With him were his helper Juan and another newcomer to the "digs," Carlos.

Professor Alvarez shook Steve's hand. "Glad to meet you, young man. This is my right-hand man, Juan. This is Carlos. He wants to learn, too. He has come all the way from Panama City."

Mules carried the supplies they would need into the rain forest. The people walked. At first the forest seemed beautiful to Steve. Then he saw he couldn't let his mind wander. Thick branches snapped back to scratch his face and hands. He tripped over twisted roots. Insects buzzed around his head. Now and then he saw a snake. Juan showed Steve how to use a big knife to clear the path. It was hard work.

"The jungle grows so fast, we have to clear a new path almost every day," Juan said.

At last they came to a clearing. Steve stopped suddenly. He could hardly believe his eyes. He saw a huge building. There were other buildings, too—or what was left of buildings. The roofs and some of the walls had caved in.

"See these patterns carved into the wall?" the

18

professor asked. "We think they are words. We are trying to learn to read them. In that way we can learn more about the Mayans."

It was a quiet spot. They were all alone deep in the jungle — except for the crowds of mosquitos.

"No wonder they call it a rain forest," said Maria. Big drops of rain had suddenly begun to

At last they came to a clearing. He could hardly believe his eyes. He saw a huge building.

fall. The sudden hard rain turned the ground quickly into mud. It was hard to walk without slipping and falling.

"It will soon stop," Juan said. Just then the sun came out. "You see, these storms do not last long at this season."

Professor Alvarez walked quickly to the largest building. "We think this is a Mayan palace," he said.

They began to climb the broken steps to the doorway. It was a long way up. Juan was first at the opening. He and Professor Alvarez went in together. Their flashlights showed strange drawings and letters carved into the walls.

Next Maria stepped through the doorway. It was almost dark. Carlos was close behind her. She stepped onto the top step and lost her balance. She screamed as she fell down the steep flight of steps into a dark world.

Carlos was the first to reach her. Steve was right behind him. Had Carlos been too quick? Maria didn't seem like the type to be careless and slip. Had someone given her a push?

Professor Alvarez handed Steve his flashlight. "Here, hold this while I see how badly she's hurt."

Maria opened her eyes. She seemed stunned.

"Maria, are you all right? Do you hurt any place?" asked the professor. He looked worried.

Maria looked up at him. "My shoulder hurts—and my ankle. Oh, I'm so sorry to be so clumsy."

Steve took hold of her hands. "Do you want to try to stand?" he asked.

"I'm sure I can stand up," Maria said. She held onto Steve's hands and pulled. Suddenly she fell back. "Oh, my ankle. I think it's sprained. I can't put any weight on it."

"Don't worry, Maria," Juan said. "We'll get you back to the base and let the nurse look at it."

Steve and Juan ran outside and got branches for a stretcher. On top of the branches they put a piece of canvas.

"I think this will work just fine," Steve said. "Let's get back inside fast. I'll feel a lot better after Maria has seen that nurse."

They carefully lifted the hurt girl onto the stretcher. Then they carried her up the inside steps of the palace out into the bright sunlight. The trip down the steep outside steps was very slow.

Professor Alvarez walked beside the stretcher. "Are you in great pain, Maria?"

She tried to smile. "It hurts a little, but I'm not

worried about that. We've lost a whole day at the digs — and just because I'm so clumsy."

The professor patted her on the head. "There will be many other days. Carlos, I think you and I ought to take a turn with the stretcher. Juan and Steve must be getting tired."

"OK," said Carlos. Just then Steve thought he saw a small knife in Carlos' hand. Before he could be sure, Carlos put the knife and another object into his jacket pocket.

The walk back seemed to take hours. They took turns carrying the stretcher and keeping the insects away from Maria. At last they reached the dam base and turned Maria over to the nurse.

The secrets of the strange palace would have to wait for a few more days.

The next day Steve stopped in to see Maria just as the doctor was leaving. The nurse had asked the doctor to drive out from Avila to be sure Maria was all right.

"Young man," the doctor said to Steve, "I want you to see that this young lady stays in bed for at least four days. And then she should be quiet for another two or three days. No hiking through the rain forest for a week!"

"I'll keep an eye on her, doctor," Steve said.

The doctor began putting things into his case.

"The jungle is not a healthy place," he said. "Bites from the insects and snakes can be deadly. Also, the Mayan ruins are old and weak. You never know when one might fall down. You were very lucky you were not hurt worse, Maria."

"I know," answered Maria. "And I'll be careful. I promise."

Bill stopped in to see Maria, too. He brought three books on Mayan history. "Here, Maria, maybe this will make the time go fast. How are you feeling?"

"I'm feeling fine, Mr. Marshall. Thank you for the books," smiled Maria.

"Glad to hear it," Bill said. "I worry about you and Steve and the others. You may be poking around in something you don't understand."

"Professor Alvarez will see that we're OK," Maria answered.

Bill frowned. "Professor Alvarez is a fine man and a good teacher. I have great respect for him. But most people here feel that Mayan ruins belong to them. They don't like strangers snooping around."

The next day Professor Alvarez came by. He was glad to see that Maria was better. He was eager to share some news.

"A very old Mayan stone has just been found,"

he said. "It seems to tell us a lot that we didn't learn from the famous *Book of the Mayans!*"

The professor turned to Steve. "You probably don't know it, Steve. The *Book of the Mayans* was found many years ago. It is not really a book. It's several pieces of stone with Mayan writing on them. We have learned almost everything we know about the Mayans from it."

"No, I didn't know that," Steve said. "Where are these stones? I'd like to see them."

Professor Alvarez stroked his beard. "So would a lot of other people. They are kept under lock and key at the Avila Museum."

Maria looked excited. "Where is the new stone?" she asked.

"It's at the university," answered the professor. "Some of our people are working on it. They will try to put it into a language that we can understand. I took a quick look at it the other day. There's something in it about a great king."

"I wonder if that is the same king my father told me about," Steve said. "That's the guy who led the Mayan people to their peak of riches."

"As yet we do not know," said Professor Alvarez. "But, of course, now I am most eager to return to the palace. It must hold many secrets."

After Professor Alvarez left, Steve pulled up a

chair near Maria's bed. "Do you want to play cards?" he asked.

"Oh, let's not play anything right now," said Maria. "Let's talk about the king. I can hardly wait to get back to the digs."

Chapter 5

Inside the Palace

A few days later Professor Alvarez and the young people again walked through the rain forest.

Steve stopped chopping with his big knife for a moment and turned to Maria. "How are you doing, Maria?"

Maria mopped her damp forehead. "Just fine. But I must say I'll be glad when we get to the ruins and get the camp set up."

"Oh, darn," Steve said. "I forgot to tell my dad we were staying overnight."

"Steve!" said Maria. "He'll be worried."

Steve kept chopping. "I don't think so. By this time he knows I can take care of myself."

After they came to the ruins, it took about an hour to unload the mules and put up the tents. Then they headed for the palace. This time no one slipped or fell. Professor Alvarez led them through many small rooms and along narrow halls. He stopped often to look at drawings and letters that had been carved into the walls. Some of the old walls had caved in. Often they had to stop to clear stones and other litter from their path. Most of this work fell to Steve and Juan. Maria helped when she could. But Carlos kept getting ahead of them. He rushed into one room, then another.

"Carlos, please stay with us," Professor Alvarez said. "You might get lost—or hurt."

Carlos shrugged his shoulders. "You guys are too slow. We'll be here all day."

"I thought that was what we came for," Maria said.

Carlos kept pushing people out of the way. A few minutes later he knocked Maria into a wall in his hurry to run down some steps. Steve saw two small green objects fall out of his pocket and roll down the stairs. Carlos rushed down the steps, picked them up, and put them in a pocket.

Steve followed him. "Hey, Carlos, you're too rough. Cut it out!"

Just then Juan called from the top of the stairs. "Come quickly. The professor has something he wants us to see."

They quickly ran up the steps and followed

Juan into a large room they had not seen before. Maria was already there with the professor. The room was the most beautiful one they had seen. It was in better shape than most of the other rooms. The walls still stood. The stone floor still gleamed. Carvings of great beauty reached from floor to ceiling.

Professor Alvarez was excited. "Look at the holes in the floor at the end of the room. They were put there on purpose. See how evenly spaced they are. I think we've stumbled on something."

They looked at the holes carefully. The biggest one was in the middle. It seemed to be covered with a slab.

"Look at the carving on that slab," Professor Alvarez said. "It's a treasure. We must remove it very carefully. Get out the tools."

It took almost an hour to remove the slab.

"Look, more steps!" said the professor. "Follow me."

Going down the steps was not easy. Each step was covered with litter and dust.

Steve sneezed. "And to think I hate to clean my room," he said.

"Many of these things were put here on purpose," said Professor Alvarez. "The people who built this didn't want anyone to get through. That means there is something important hidden below."

Slowly the odds and ends were cleared away. Slowly they moved downward, step by step. Finally they reached the bottom. They looked at one another. Their way was blocked by another

"Look at the carving on that slab. It's a treasure. We must remove it very carefully."

huge slab.

"I hate to say it, but I'm getting tired," Maria said. "And my lungs are filled with dust."

"You're right," agreed Professor Alvarez. "We all need some fresh air and rest."

Once outside they all took deep breaths of the fresh air.

"I'm starved," Steve said.

"You're always starved," Maria laughed.

"That's what my dad says," he answered.

Their evening meal was a simple one. Maria made hot tea over the camp stove. After two or three cups everyone felt much better.

"Does anyone want to go for a walk?" Maria asked.

"I do," Steve said. He got up and stretched his long legs.

"Take a flashlight with you, and don't go too far," ordered Professor Alvarez. "Night comes quickly in the rain forest."

Maria and Steve walked slowly through the courtyard that was on three sides of the palace.

"I don't trust Carlos," Steve said. "He acts so strange. What's up with him?"

"Did you see the green beads he dropped?" Maria asked.

"I sure did," Steve replied. "I didn't know you

had seen them, too."

"I think I know that they are," Maria said. "They looked like jade earrings. They were worn only by the high priests and the royal family of Maya. They are very rare and very valuable."

"What do you think we should do about it, Maria?" Steve asked.

She thought for a moment. Then she said, "I don't really know. Maybe we should wait and see what happens. Maybe Carlos will be better tomorrow."

Steve kicked one of the stones in his path. "Maybe. But if he is, I'll be surprised. But then this place is full of surprises."

Chapter 6

The Secret
of the Palace

Jungle birds woke the group up early the next morning. It was going to be another hot day.

"Let's start before it gets too hot," Professor Alvarez said. "Steve, I want you to keep track of the time. We must start back by two or three o'clock."

Their walk through the palace rooms and halls seemed easier this morning. They knew where they were going. They knew what tools they would need. In fifteen minutes they were once again at the bottom of the stairs. They all stared at the heavy stone.

"It looks as if it has been here for hundreds of years," Maria said.

"It has," agreed the professor.

"OK, amigos, let's get to work," Juan said.

Steve, Juan, and Carlos rolled up their sleeves and got out the prying tools. The professor and

Maria pointed the flashlights on their work. It was more than an hour before the heavy slab gave way. They all looked through the opening. Before them was a long hallway. It was bare. No carvings of any kind.

"If there's another slab at the end of this hall, I'm going back for dynamite," Steve said. "Just kidding," he added when he saw the professor's frown.

They climbed through the opening and walked down the long hall. At the end of it they found a large rock bowl. In it were jade beads, some dishes, and a set of jade earrings.

"I think this must be an offering to the Mayan gods," Professor Alvarez said. "What isn't clear to me is why the offering was put in this place."

He carefully lifted the objects and gave them to Maria. They all waited while she carefully marked each piece and placed them gently in her sack.

"Now what?" asked Carlos.

Steve smiled. "Another wall. What else? I wish we had some of my dad's heavy digging equipment here."

Professor Alvarez looked shocked. "Oh, no. We must be very careful. Nothing must be damaged."

"I know. I know. Just kidding, Professor," Steve said. "Let's get on with it."

Even Carlos did his full share of the work. He seemed lots more cheerful after they had found the jade objects.

More than an hour passed before the wall caved in. They cleared away the stones and dust. Another wall!

"This is too much," Steve said. "At the rate we're going, we'll be here all summer."

"Wait!" Juan said. He got down on his knees and began to dust off a low door frame. It was barely three feet high.

"See?" Juan said. "This is the arch the Mayans always used in their buildings. It has a triangle on the top. I'm sure this is a doorway."

Steve put his hand on the small door and pushed. It was stuck.

Professor Alvarez moved in beside him. "Let me look. Yes. I think if we just chip away at the edges, we can get it loose."

They took turns chipping away at the stone door. It had been perfectly fitted to the opening.

"Hey," Steve called. "I think I felt it move a little. Juan, let's push together."

Juan moved quickly to his side. Together they gave a big push. The stone fell backwards into a room. On hands and knees Steve and Juan peered through the opening.

"Give me your flashlight, Maria," Juan said. He beamed the light into the room. "It looks like a huge church."

One by one they crawled through the small opening. The room was filled with beautiful carvings. On the floor in one corner was a large slab. It was made of limestone. It sparkled when the light from the flashlight hit it.

The figure of a man was carved into the top of the slab. He was wearing jewels and a kind of crown. He was about six feet long. Near his head were carved figures.

The professor bent over the slab and ran his fingers along its edge. "This slab is not solid," he said. "Let's try to pry it open."

"Oh, oh, here we go again," thought Steve. But this time he was wrong. They were able to pry the slab up easily. They laid it carefully to one side. Inside was another box just a little smaller covered with jewels.

"Let's lift off the top," Professor Alvarez said. "Easy! Easy! We don't want to crack it."

The top was not heavy, and they laid it on top of the slab. Everyone bent over to see what was inside.

"Wow!" Steve said. "Look at *that!*"

The professor fell to his knees. "At last," he said, "we've found it. The king! The king!"

Inside the box was the skeleton of a tall man. There were ten jade rings on the ten finger bones. One skeleton hand held a round jade piece. It was about three inches across. In the other hand was a jade cube about the same size. Around the skeleton were many pieces of jade jewelry — beads and bracelets. There was a brightly-colored mask. There were pieces of pottery. What a find!

Professor Alvarez's eyes were bright with tears. He had trouble speaking. "All of these things were buried only with kings. I know this is the king. How wonderful! After hundreds of years, he is going to teach us so much about his life and the lives of his people."

"Not just yet," Carlos said. His voice sounded like ice. They all turned and looked at him. He was pointing a gun at the professor's forehead.

"What in the world . . . " began Maria.

"Shut up!" said Carlos.

Steve started moving toward him. "You can't get away with this, Carlos."

"Stay away from me. You bet I can get away with it. I've been planning this for a long time."

Carlos' voice was angry.

They all stared at one another. Now what?

Carlos knew exactly what he was doing. "Steve, you take that rope and tie up the professor and Juan. Maria, you pack these bags with all the jewels they will hold."

"Then what?" Steve asked.

"Not just yet," Carlos said. He was pointing a gun at the professor's head.

"Then I'll tie you up," growled Carlos. "I'll take Maria and the mules back to the dam site. I'll let her go when we get there. She can send someone back to get you. My friends have a car waiting for me. We'll be far away by the time you all are freed."

Juan looked at the ceiling above Carlos' head. "Look out, Carlos!" he shouted.

"Don't try that old trick on me," Carlos started to say. Then he fell to the ground. He had been knocked out by a large stone. It had broken loose from the ceiling.

Steve moved fast. He picked up Carlos' gun. "Now it's your turn to be tied up, old buddy," he said.

The professor was pale. "What are we going to do with him?"

Steve grinned. "That's easy, Professor. We'll tie him up and sling him over the back of one of the mules. It will be a rough trip back to the dam site, but we can make it. Maybe Juan can go on ahead and bring some help. I wouldn't want to bump into any of Carlos' pals."

It took a long time to drag Carlos' limp body up all the steep stairs, through the halls and rooms. At last they were outside.

At first it was hard to see in the bright

sunlight. And then—what was this? Soldiers were coming through the courtyard. They were wearing the uniform of Prima Vera.

"Hooray," Steve shouted. "The marines have landed!"

Chapter 7

The Treasures
of Prima Vera

The next day Steve and Bill Marshall were talking in their room. Steve was glad it was Sunday. He and his father could have some time together at last.

Steve stretched out on the bed. "That Carlos was nothing but a rotten grave robber."

"He was a lot more than that," Bill said. "The Avila police say he has a long record."

"I believe it," Steve answered. "He sure knew how to handle that gun. But stealing old Mayan treasures seems a little far out to me."

"He was only a small link in a big chain, Steve," his father said. "He worked for a gang of crooks. They have members all over the world. Stealing a country's treasures is big business to them. It goes on all the time, and it's too bad."

"Did they catch any of the others?" Steve asked.

"Not yet," Bill said. "I have a hunch that Carlos may change his mind and start talking. They are going to offer him less time in jail if he turns in some of his pals."

"Say, Dad, I never thanked you for sending in the army," grinned Steve.

"Well, I got worried when you didn't come back that night. I talked to one of my friends here. He's in the army. He's the one who sent out the soldiers," Bill said.

Steve got up from the bed. "I feel bad that I forgot to tell you we were going to be away overnight. I didn't mean to worry you."

"I know you didn't," his father answered. "And it's OK—this time. But don't make a habit of it. I might not always have an army to send after you. Now, would you like to walk over to the social hall?"

"Sure," Steve said.

They found Maria and Juan and Professor Alvarez in the social hall. They were sipping iced tea and talking.

The professor stood up and shook hands with Steve and his father. "Thanks to my young friends here, the treasures from the palace are safe. You will be able to see them in the national museum in Avila. And there will be men to guard them twenty-four hours a day!"

"Have you finished your work here, Professor?" Steve asked.

"Oh, no. There is still a lot to do." His eyes twinkled. "Perhaps you all have had enough and will not want to go back with me."

"I'm game," grinned Steve. "How about you, Maria—and Juan?"

Their quick smiles were all the answer the professor needed. "Good," he said. "And I have more news. The president of Prima Vera would like to hold a dinner for you before you leave our country. Do you think you would enjoy that?"

The three young people beamed.

"Wow!" Steve said. "That sounds great. Could my father come, too?"

"But, of course," smiled Professor Alvarez. "He would be most welcome."

Later Steve and Bill walked slowly back to their trailer.

Steve cleared his throat. "Dad, I think I owe you an apology. I was mad when I got your letter. I really didn't want to come to Prima Vera at all."

His father patted him on the back. "I know, Steve. I was afraid to let you make up your mind. I knew you would say no. So I played the heavy and made you come."

"Well, I'm sure glad you did," Steve said. "I feel sorry for Brad and the gang stuck at that dull camp all summer."

"You're going to have a lot to tell them when you get back," Bill said.

"I sure will. I wonder if they will believe me,"

"You're going to have a lot to tell them when you get back".

said Steve.

"As a matter of fact, I think you are going to have some proof," his father said. "Professor Alvarez told me that the president of Prima Vera is going to make you and Maria honorary citizens. They are going to give you the key to the city of Avila. Not a bad trophy to take home with you."

"No kidding?" Mark grinned from ear to ear. "Wait till they see that. By the way, Dad, what are you doing next summer?"